WELCOME TO
PASSPORT TO READING
A beginning reader's ticket to a brand-new world!

Every book in this program is designed to build read-along and read-alone skills, level by level, through engaging and enriching stories. As the reader turns each page, he or she will become more confident with new vocabulary, sight words, and comprehension.

These PASSPORT TO READING levels will help you choose the perfect book for every reader.

READING TOGETHER
Read short words in simple sentence structures together to begin a reader's journey.

READING OUT LOUD
Encourage developing readers to sound out words in more complex stories with simple vocabulary.

READING INDEPENDENTLY
Newly independent readers gain confidence reading more complex sentences with higher word counts.

READY TO READ MORE
Readers prepare for chapter books with fewer illustrations and longer paragraphs.

This book features sight words from the educator-supported Dolch Sight Words List. This encourages the reader to recognize commonly used vocabulary words, increasing reading speed and fluency.

For more information, please visit passporttoreadingbooks.com.

Enjoy the journey!

TRANS FORMERS

Roll Out and Read Adventures

LB

LITTLE, BROWN AND COMPANY

New York   Boston

Little, Brown and Company

Hachette Book Group
237 Park Avenue, New York, NY 10017
Visit our website at lb-kids.com

Little, Brown and Company is a division of Hachette Book Group, Inc.
The Little, Brown name and logo are trademarks of Hachette Book Group, Inc.

The publisher is not responsible for websites (or their content)
that are not owned by the publisher.

First Edition: April 2014

Meet the Autobots and *Meet the Decepticons* originally published
in 2007 by HarperCollins Publishers
I Am Optimus Prime and *Rise of the Decepticons* originally published
in 2009 by HarperCollins Publishers
The Lost Autobot and *Optimus Prime's Friends and Foes* originally published
in 2011 by Little, Brown and Company

ISBN 978-0-316-20743-0

Library of Congress Control Number: 2013950443

10 9 8 7 6 5 4 3 2 1

SC

Printed in China

LICENSED BY:

Passport to Reading titles are leveled by independent reviewers applying the standards developed by Irene Fountas and Gay Su Pinnell in *Matching Books to Readers: Using Leveled Books in Guided Reading*, Heinemann, 1999.

TRANS FORMERS

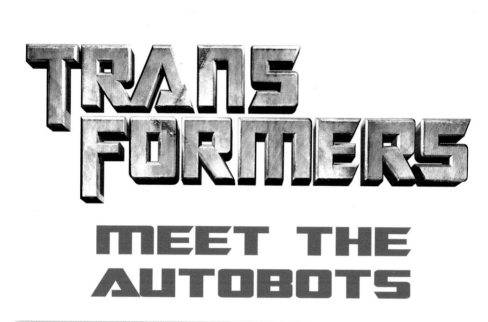

TRANSFORMERS

MEET THE AUTOBOTS

Adapted by Jennifer Frantz
Illustrations by Guido Guidi
Based on the Screenplay by Roberto Orci & Alex Kurtzman
from a story by Roberto Orci & Alex Kurtzman and John Rogers

The Autobots are Transformers.

They fight for good and freedom.

Their planet, Cybertron,

was destroyed in a battle

with the evil Decepticons.

Now they have landed on Earth!

The Autobots are searching
for a new home.
They are also looking
for something else.

MISSION

To find the AllSpark,

the core of all robot life force,

before the Decepticons do.

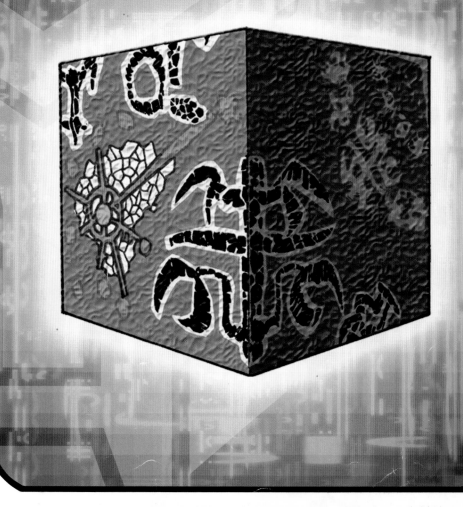

Bumblebee seeks out
a little human help.

He picks up some new friends,
Sam and Mikaela.

Bumblebee gets a cool new shape, too!
Bumblebee is happy
when his friend Sam smiles.

But danger is just around the corner.

This is not a real cop on patrol!

Bumblebee transforms

into a supersonic bad-guy blaster.

With a fast move,

he saves his human pals

from a deadly Decepticon.

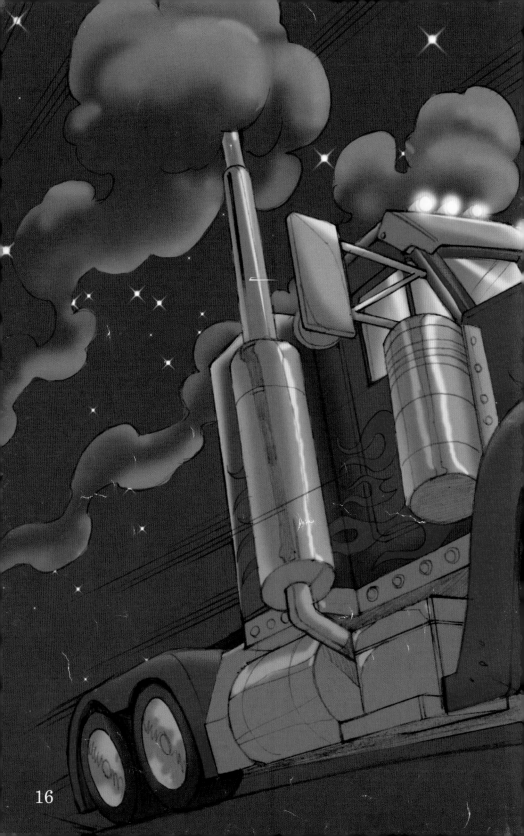

A huge truck charges
through the darkness.
But this is no ordinary truck.

It is Optimus Prime—
leader of the Autobots!
He is strong and good.
Optimus Prime calls
his Autobot friends.

Jazz is Optimus Prime's
right-hand man.
He is loyal and brave.

No one can top Jazz's speed and style.

Ironhide knows all about fighting.

He is one tough Autobot!

He is always ready to blast his way out of danger.

Ratchet can see trouble
a mile away.
He has X-ray vision!

Ratchet is the rescue truck.

He is always there to help a friend.

"Autobots, roll out!"
Optimus Prime orders.

It's time to find the AllSpark
and stop the evil Decepticons.

27

Yikes!

The Autobots are trapped.

But it is nothing a powerful pulse blast

cannot handle!

Using a little teamwork,
they get rid of the threat.

Optimus Prime is under attack.

He thinks fast.

He dives for cover.

No one will find him under this bridge!

The Autobots battle the Decepticons
for the AllSpark.
Bumblebee takes a bad hit,
but he will be okay.

Optimus Prime swoops in to save Sam.

And Sam saves the AllSpark!

Optimus Prime fights to the end.

Optimus Prime and the Autobots
have saved Earth.
In return, the Autobots
have a new planet to call home.

They will live on Earth—

hidden safely in the human world.

Optimus Prime stands quietly.

"Life is good," he thinks.

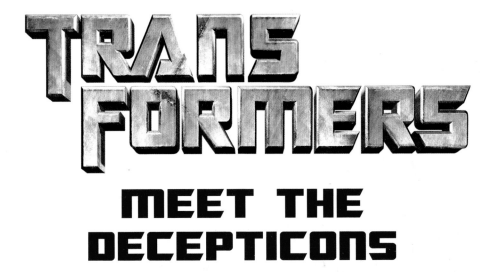

MEET THE
DECEPTICONS

Adapted by Jennifer Frantz
Illustrations by Guido Guidi
Based on the Screenplay by Roberto Orci & Alex Kurtzman
from a story by Roberto Orci & Alex Kurtzman and John Rogers

Evil alien robots called Decepticons
have landed on Earth.
They are from the planet Cybertron.

The Decepticons fight
to take over the universe.
They will not stop until they win.
And their next battle
will take place here on Earth.

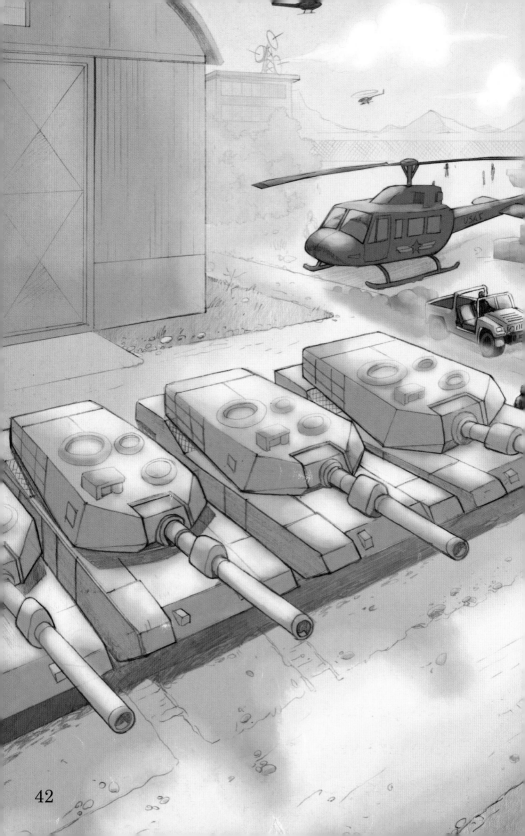

The Decepticons are Transformers.
They are robots that hide among us.
They pretend to be regular machines.
They are very tricky and very bad.

A friendly chopper comes in for a landing.

But that chopper is not what it seems.

It turns into a Decepticon named Blackout!

Blackout crushes steel cars.

His blasts wipe out anything in his way.

Blackout is full of nasty surprises.

He carries a robot named Skorponok.

Skorponok digs through the desert sand.

He can sense anything that moves.

He hunts like a scorpion.

He is dangerous.

Frenzy is a Decepticon, too.

He is very tricky.

He can turn into a radio or a boom box.

When he is a robot,

he can shoot metal discs.

Frenzy wants to make big trouble.
He shuts down all the computers
with his terrible scream.

Barricade is another bad guy.

He can transform into a police car.

Frenzy wants to come along.

He turns into the car's CD player.

They drive the streets
looking for trouble.

Megatron is the most powerful
of all Decepticons.
He is a metal giant.
He feeds on energy.
Megatron will not rest
until he finds the AllSpark.
It is the Transformers' life force.
Megatron wants it all for himself!

Megatron transforms into
a supersonic jet.
He blasts off on his evil mission.

Megatron finds what he is looking for.

It is the AllSpark!

He sends a signal

to the other Decepticons.

Decepticons come
from all over
to help their leader.
The Decepticon named Starscream
jets through the sky.

Bonecrusher and Brawl
rumble over the ground.

The Decepticons unite.

Blackout

Skorponok

Barricade

Frenzy

Together they are a deadly force.

Starscream

Bonecrusher

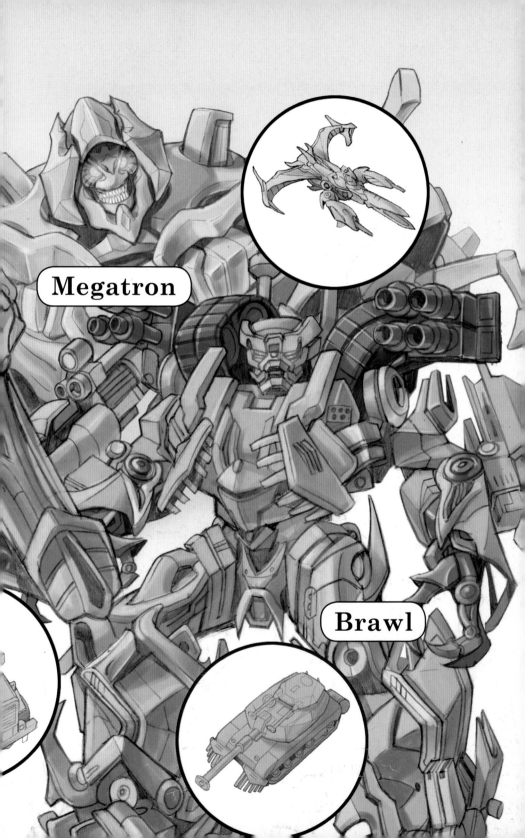

Megatron

Brawl

Who can stop Megatron
and his Decepticon army?
The Autobots!

Autobots are good Transformers.

Their leader is Optimus Prime.

They want to save Earth

from the evil Decepticons.

The battle for the AllSpark
and for planet Earth is on.
The metal giants lock in battle.

Megatron takes a hit!

The Decepticons lose this battle!

They flee the planet.

For now the Earth is safe.

TRANSFORMERS
REVENGE OF THE FALLEN

I Am Optimus Prime

Adapted by Jennifer Frantz
Illustrations by Guido Guidi

Based on the Screenplay by
Ehren Kruger & Alex Kurtzman & Roberto Orci

Optimus Prime is the brave leader
of the Autobots.
They are robots in disguise!

Optimus is not just any Bot.
He is the last of the great Primes,
a line of noble robots.
They come from
the planet Cybertron.

Like all true Primes,

Optimus fights for what is right.

Here on planet Earth,
Optimus Prime
is a friend to humans.

Side by side,
humans and Autobots battled Megatron
and his evil Decepticons.

And Optimus Prime has a new enemy.
The enemy's name is The Fallen.

The Fallen is even more evil
and powerful than Megatron.
He feeds on energy,
growing stronger and stronger.
The Fallen wants to absorb
the sun's energy
and destroy planet Earth.

Optimus Prime must
stop The Fallen.
But he is not alone!

The brave Autobots are ready to do whatever their leader asks.

Look out, Decepticons!
The Twins might look little,
but they are double trouble.

Ironhide and Optimus Prime
make a great team.
Together they defeat the evil Demolisher.

Bumblebee is a loyal Bot.
He will go anywhere
to help a friend.

Sideswipe is a fearless fighter.

He will do anything

for Optimus Prime.

The battle is on!
The Autobots face off
against the Decepticons.

Optimus Prime is ready to rumble!

Bumblebee blasts
a bulldozing Decepticon!
Bumblebee is small and fast.

Bumblebee has never fought better.

He wins this battle!

The Twins take on
the deadly Devastator.

This giant Bot
is bad news!

In the end,
Optimus Prime sends The Fallen
screaming into space.
The sun is saved.

Optimus made the Earth
safe from Decepticons.
At least for now.

Rise of the Decepticons

Adapted by Jennifer Frantz

Illustrations by Marcelo Matere

Based on the Screenplay by
Ehren Kruger & Alex Kurtzman & Roberto Orci

The evil Megatron lost
his last battle
with Optimus Prime,
the leader of the Autobots.

Megatron is the leader
of the Decepticons.
Decepticons and Autobots
are sworn enemies.

Megatron is deep down
at the bottom of the sea.
His body is rusty and broken.
He used to be dangerous.
Now he lies still.

Humans do not want Megatron
to rise up again.
The Navy watches over him
with submarines.

Megatron's Decepticon forces
want to get their leader back.
Soundwave hacks into
the Navy computers.

Soundwave finds all the top secret
information he needs.
Now the Decepticons can make a plan.

The Decepticons must get
the AllSpark shard.
It was the source of
Megatron's energy.

The shard is in a locked vault.

Ravage outsmarts the humans.

He gets the shard!

Now that they have the shard,
the Decepticons are ready
to go to their leader.

The Decepticons get past
the submarines.
The evil Bots find Megatron.

The Doctor is a nimble Bot.
Using his jointed arms,
the Doctor puts the shard
into Megatron.

Megatron bursts to life!

He is back and he is bad.

Now the good guys have
to watch out.
The battle for Earth
has never been harder.

Megatron is not alone.

His Decepticon army is by his side.

There are many
dangerous Decepticons.
Starscream is a supersonic warrior.

Devastator is one MEGA-bot!

He is a scary foe.

But the most evil Decepticon of all
is The Fallen.
The Fallen has been asleep
for ages.
Now he is back, and he is stronger
than ever!

The Autobots
and their human friends
prepare for one hard fight.

115

Luckily, the Autobots have
two secret weapons.
Wheels and Jetfire are Decepticons
who changed sides.

Now they fight for good
with Optimus Prime
and the Autobots.

Wheels is small,
but he is as brave
as the biggest Bot.

Jetfire is old,

but he is still very powerful.

He is also very wise.

Can the Autobots beat
the Decepticons once again?

Or will Megatron and The Fallen be too powerful?

Only one thing is for sure:
Optimus Prime and his Autobots
will never give up!

TRANS FORMERS

DARK OF THE MOON

THE LOST AUTOBOT

Adapted by KATHARINE TURNER

Illustrations by GUIDO GUIDI

Based on the Screenplay by EHREN KRUGER

Long ago, in outer space,
a race of alien robots
lived in peace on a planet
called Cybertron.

The planet began to run out of energy.
The robots fought one another
for control of the planet.
The war destroyed their home.

The Autobots fought for freedom
against the power-hungry Decepticons.
The Decepticons were winning.

So the Autobot leader flew
into space on a secret mission
to find a new home.
The spaceship was called the Ark.
It was the Autobots' last hope.

Many years later, on Earth,
American astronauts went to the moon.
The astronauts found something!
They saw an alien spaceship!

The astronauts climbed inside
the old spaceship.

They were on board the Autobots' Ark.

The Ark had crashed into the moon.
It never completed its mission.

"Houston, we are inside the ship,"
one astronaut said into his radio.
"But there are no signs of life."

When the Ark was lost,
the Autobots fled Cybertron.
Led by Optimus Prime,
they came to Earth to live with humans.

The Decepticons followed.

They want to take over Earth.

But the Autobots and their friends

have stopped them so far.

The Autobots work with humans
to protect Earth.
They go on a mission to Russia,
where they uncover a secret.

The Russians had been to the moon, too.

They had taken a piece of the Ark.

Optimus Prime knows at once

that it came from the Autobot spaceship.

Optimus is shocked.

He did not know that humans

found the Ark many years ago.

Suddenly, a giant drill creature
comes up through the ground
carrying a Decepticon called Shockwave!
He wants to steal the piece of the Ark.

Shockwave blasts the Autobots
with his cannon.
An arm of the drill beast
grabs the piece of the Ark.

Optimus turns his trailer into a shield.
He fires back at Shockwave
and slices the driller.
The Decepticon retreats.

Back in America,

Optimus demands to know more

about the mission to the moon.

He is angry that he was not told before.

The head of national intelligence
tells Optimus the mission was top secret.
Only a few people knew
about the moon trip and the Ark.

Optimus must go to the moon.

The Autobots need to see the ship.

Maybe they will find

the leader who was lost.

The Autobots roll out.

The Transformers land on the moon and find the wreckage of the Ark.

The ship is torn up from the crash.

Inside the spaceship,

Optimus finds a secret door.

It is locked.

He enters a code.

The door opens.

There are no signs of life.

Optimus finds a lost Transformer.

It is Sentinel Prime.

He was the powerful Autobot leader

back on Cybertron.

He and Optimus were friends.

Sentinel left Cybertron in the Ark so long ago!

There is no glow in his eyes now.

The Autobots take him to Earth.

As the current leader
of the Autobots,
Optimus Prime protects
the Matrix of Leadership.

The Matrix can bring
Transformers back to life.
Optimus opens his chest,
and a beam of light hits Sentinel.

The Matrix lights Sentinel's Spark.

It brings Sentinel Prime back to life.

Sentinel wakes up.

He is confused.

"Where am I?" he asks.

Optimus explains that
the Ark crashed on the moon long ago.
The Autobots lost the war
and left Cybertron.

Sentinel is happy to see Optimus.

The Autobots are happy Sentinel will help them defend their new home on Earth.

TRANSFORMERS

DARK OF THE MOON

OPTIMUS PRIME'S FRIENDS AND FOES

Adapted by KATHARINE TURNER

Illustrations by GUIDO GUIDI

Based on the Screenplay by EHREN KRUGER

Transformers are alien robots
from a planet called Cybertron.
They can change into machines,
such as cars and trucks.

Optimus Prime changes
into a big semitruck with a trailer.
Optimus Prime is an Autobot
who wants peace.

The Autobots have made
a new home on Earth.
They help their human friends
protect the planet.

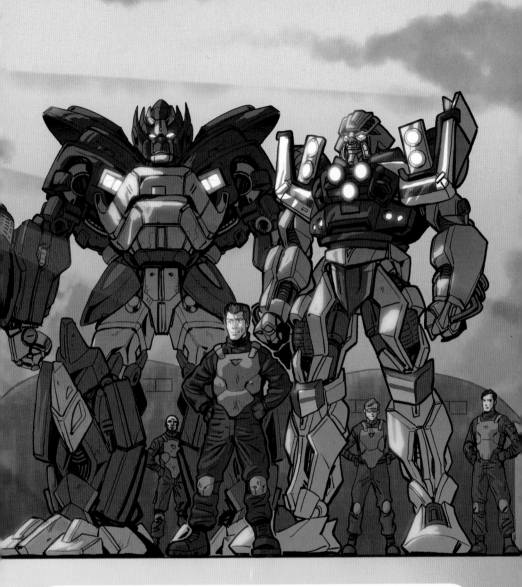

Some Autobots came to Earth
with Optimus Prime many years ago.
Bumblebee, Ironhide,
and Ratchet are his friends.

Sam Witwicky was Optimus Prime's
first human friend.
Colonel Lennox is their friend, too.

Sam and Lennox help Optimus
and the Autobots battle
evil Transformers called Decepticons.

New Transformers have come to Earth
to join Optimus and the Autobots.
Wheeljack is one of them.
His vehicle mode is a dark blue car.

Wheeljack likes to invent things.
He made grapple gloves that fire hooks
to help Lennox and his soldiers
climb walls and large robots.

Mirage is a new Autobot, too.

He is one of the good guys.

He changes into a red sports car
and likes to drive very fast.
Mirage can appear to be invisible
to confuse the bad guys.

The Wreckers work as a team.

The three Autobots

like to change into race cars.

The Wreckers are mechanics
who are helping a human named Epps
rebuild an Autobot spaceship.
They will make it fly again!

All of Optimus's friends mean a lot to him, but one friend is very special.
This Autobot was found on the moon!

Sentinel Prime was the Autobots' leader
back on Cybertron.

He has a giant rust cannon
that can destroy metal objects.

Optimus is happy to have his friend back.

He shows Sentinel Prime

the Autobots' new home on Earth.

Some Transformers are bad guys.

They are called the Decepticons.

Their leader is Megatron.

He wants to take over Earth.

Optimus Prime and his friends have battled the Decepticons before and saved Earth.

Megatron never gives up.
He hides from the Autobots
in the sandy desert
while he plans his next attack.

There are new Decepticons on Earth who will fight. Shockwave is a smart robot with a single glowing eye.

Shockwave rides a beast
that looks like a big drill.
They can tunnel underground
to attack Optimus Prime.

Laserbeak is another Decepticon.

He looks like a bird robot.

He can change into many forms.

Laserbeak can turn into a television,
a computer, or a stereo.
He hides in plain sight
to spy on humans.

More Decepticons hide on the moon,
waiting to come to Earth
and take over the planet.

Megatron gathers his army.
He transports the robots
from the moon to Earth
for a final battle.

Who is that helping Megatron?

It is Sentinel Prime!

He has betrayed the Autobots.

Sentinel wants to rule Earth, too.

Optimus Prime feels sad
that his old friend is his new foe.
But Optimus must protect his new home.
All his friends join the battle.

Sentinel aims his cannon at Optimus.
He says, "To save our own kind,
we must take over the planet.
I did not want to betray you."

A laser blast hits Sentinel's cannon, giving Optimus a chance to grab it out of the robot's hands. "You betrayed yourself," says Optimus.

Optimus Prime's foes are defeated,
and his friends are safe.
Optimus has won this battle.
Earth is safe once more!

TRANS FORMERS
P R I M E
PASSPORT **2** TO READING
Meet Team Prime

TRANS FORMERS
P R I M E
PASSPORT **2** TO READING
Decepticon
in Disguise

TRANSFORMERS PRIME

Attack of the Scraplets!

TRANSFORMERS PRIME

Autobots versus Zombies

TRANS
FORMERS
PRIME

Optimus Prime
and the Secret
Mission

TRANSFORMERS
PRIME
BEAST
HUNTERS

Optimus Prime
versus
Predaking

TRANSFORMERS RESCUE BOTS

The Mystery of the Pirate Bell

TRANSFORMERS RESCUE BOTS

Return of the Dinobot

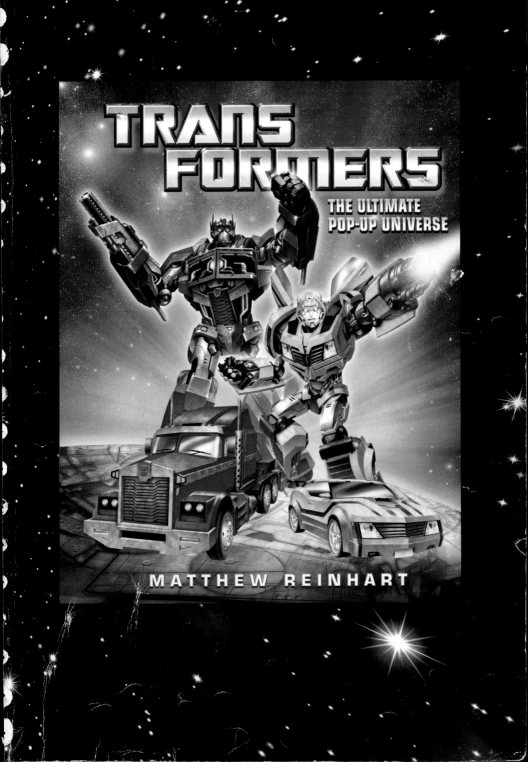

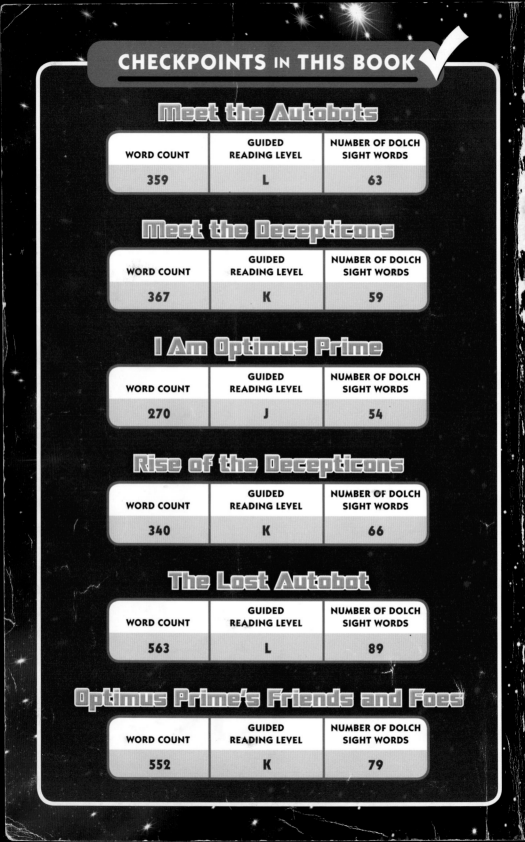

CHECKPOINTS in THIS BOOK ✓

Meet the Autobots

WORD COUNT	GUIDED READING LEVEL	NUMBER OF DOLCH SIGHT WORDS
359	L	63

Meet the Decepticons

WORD COUNT	GUIDED READING LEVEL	NUMBER OF DOLCH SIGHT WORDS
367	K	59

I Am Optimus Prime

WORD COUNT	GUIDED READING LEVEL	NUMBER OF DOLCH SIGHT WORDS
270	J	54

Rise of the Decepticons

WORD COUNT	GUIDED READING LEVEL	NUMBER OF DOLCH SIGHT WORDS
340	K	66

The Lost Autobot

WORD COUNT	GUIDED READING LEVEL	NUMBER OF DOLCH SIGHT WORDS
563	L	89

Optimus Prime's Friends and Foes

WORD COUNT	GUIDED READING LEVEL	NUMBER OF DOLCH SIGHT WORDS
552	K	79